Hello!

In our house we've always been prepared for big storms; blizzards or hurricanes, we're ready for the worst. But when Hurricanes Katrina and Rita tore through the South, I realized that we weren't completely prepared; we had to make emergency plans for our dog.

Disasters are scary times for human beings, but at least we can listen to weather updates and know what to expect. Pets are often terrified by dangerous weather. The changes in atmospheric pressure affect them much more than us, and howling winds and rising water can send them into a panic.

Our pets rely on us to be there for them in good times and in bad. We now have an emergency supply of food and medicine for our dog, and we've figured out what we would do with her if we were ever evacuated. I hope you will be bold and brave enough to do the same thing for your pet!

Laurie Halse Anderson

THE VET VOLUNTEER BOOKS

Fight for Life
Homeless
Trickster
Manatee Blues
Say Good-bye
Storm Rescue

VET
VOLUNTEERS

STORM RESCUE

LAURIE HALSE ANDERSON

SCHOLASTIC INC.
New York Toronto London Auckland
Sydney Mexico City New Delhi Hong Kong

Acknowledgments

Thanks to Kimberly Michels, D.V.M.

ISBN: 978-0-545-11038-9

12 11 10 9 8 7 6 5 4 3 2   10 11 12 13 14 15/0

Printed in the U.S.A.   40

First Scholastic Book Club printing, January 2010

To Catherine Hapka

Chapter One

· · · · · · · · · · ·

What are you trying to do, Sunita?" Maggie MacKenzie asks as she flops down onto the deck beside me. "Turn that cat into a dog?"

I tuck my long, dark hair behind one ear and grin at Maggie. "No way," I say. "I like Lucy just the way she is!"

I toss the small, squishy ball I'm holding. "Mwaaawr!" Lucy cries, and pounces on the ball, batting it with one paw as she rolls over onto her back. I expect her to twist around and whap the ball again. Instead, she just lies there for a second with all four paws straight up in the air.

Maggie giggles. "I guess it's too hot for playing ball today. Sherlock is acting even lazier than usual, too."

"I guess." I stare at Lucy, a little surprised. Even though she's thirteen years old, she's almost always as playful as a kitten—not like Maggie's basset hound, Sherlock Holmes, who is pretty lazy.

Finally, Lucy rolls the rest of the way over, halfheartedly bats the ball—and gets tangled up in her leash.

I reach for her. "Lucy, you love playing ball, remember?" I say, untangling her. Lucy's leash and the harness it's attached to are blue, just like her eyes. She blinks at me, then rubs her head against my chin to say thank you.

Lucy is one of my favorite patients here at Dr. Mac's Place, where I'm a volunteer. She's a seal-point Siamese cat—that's a breed of cat with a light-colored body and dark brown fur on its legs, tail, and face. The darker areas are called points.

I love pet-sitting for Lucy when her owner, Mrs. Clark, goes out of town—even though Lucy is a big responsibility. She has diabetes. That means her body doesn't produce a special protein called insulin. It turns food into glucose, a sugar that gives the body energy. So Lucy needs an injection of insulin twice a day to help regulate her body's glucose level. Dr. Mac taught me how to give her the shots.

I set Lucy down. "Mrrwowrr!" she says loudly. That's another thing about Siamese cats. They're really talkative.

"Just goes to show." Maggie blows a few tendrils of red hair off her face as she watches Lucy stalk the ball again. Maggie's face is so red from the summer heat that her freckles hardly show at all. "There's no point putting a leash on a cat."

I don't bother to reply to that. It's too hot to argue. It's the Saturday before Labor Day, and the day of the clinic's annual picnic. Every year, all the clinic's patients are invited to celebrate the end of summer. Their owners are invited, too, of course.

Maggie's grandmother owns the clinic. Her name is Dr. J.J. MacKenzie, but most people just call her Dr. Mac. Maggie and her cousin Zoe call her Gran, though aside from her white hair, nobody would guess she was old enough to be a grandmother. She's tall, wears bright T-shirts from The Gap, and never seems to stop moving.

Right now she's with her partner, Dr. Gabe, talking to some picnic guests with a pair of panting poodles.

Personally, I'm glad Mrs. Clark taught her to walk on a leash. Lucy is the only cat at the whole picnic except for Dr. Mac's big orange cat, Socrates. One woman brought her cockatoo and is walking around with the big white bird perched on her shoulder. Another owner has a pet rat peeking out of his shirt pocket. But otherwise, everywhere I look I see dogs, dogs, dogs. There must be thirty or forty dogs of all shapes and sizes in the clinic's grassy, fenced-in backyard. I'm glad that Lucy and I are up on the deck, out of the way.

Don't get me wrong. I like almost all the animals that come to Dr. Mac's Place—dogs, ferrets, rabbits, pigs, snakes, horses, hamsters, birds, and more. But I've always loved cats the most. There's something about the way they move. Or maybe it's the way they look at you, like they know everything you're thinking.

I've wanted a cat for so long that it's hard to believe I finally have one of my own. Her name is Mittens, and I helped rescue her and her kittens. My mother and father made me find new homes for the kittens when they were old enough, but I got to keep Mittens.

Having a cat is a lot of responsibility—I have to remember to keep her food and water bowls filled and clean out the litter box every day. But having a cat is also just as wonderful as I always thought it would be. Mittens nuzzles my chin to wake me up in the morning, warms my lap while I read, and greets me at the door when I come home. What more could you ask for?

I watch Lucy hunch down and wiggle her backside as she stares at her ball intently. "My father says today is a triple-H day," I tell Maggie. "It's hazy, hot, and humid."

Maggie nods and glances around. "Yeah. I'm glad we put out all those extra water bowls around the yard," she says. "It would be easy for a dog to get dehydrated in this heat."

It's no surprise that Maggie is more concerned about the animals at the picnic than the people. She loves animals as much as I do—especially dogs. Maggie can train almost any dog to do almost anything. She even taught Sherlock to put his food dish in the dishwasher. When she opens the door, he pulls out the lower rack and plops the dish in. It's so cute!

"Uh-oh," Maggie says, holding out her hand and glancing up at the sky. "It's sprinkling."

A drop hits Lucy and she flinches. That's another reason I like cats. I don't like water, either—especially when I can't touch the bottom. In fact, I'm afraid of anything deeper than my bathtub.

"I hope it doesn't start raining harder and ruin the picnic. I was just about to get another hot dog," Maggie says.

"Blame it on Felix," I say, hugging Lucy to me as another drop splashes on my arm.

Maggie frowns. "Who?"

"That's the name of that hurricane that's coming up the coast," I explain, stepping back to stand under the overhang of the roof.

Maggie ducks under the roof with me and says, "Oh, right, I saw that on the news this morning. But what does Hurricane Felix have to do with us? It's way down in South Carolina or somewhere."

I'm about to answer, but just then Lucy wriggles in my arms. Letting out a little grunt, she pushes at me with her hind legs and tries to escape my grasp.

"Lucy!" I say in surprise, putting her down.

"What's up, girl?" She loves being held almost as much as she loves playing with her ball. Why is she acting so weird?

Lucy circles my legs once, shaking her wet paws after each step. Then she stands on her hind feet and hugs my leg with her two front paws.

"Told you so," I say, picking her up again.

"Typical fickle cat," Maggie kids, and pats Lucy on the head.

"Hey," David calls as he lopes up onto the deck.

"Hi," says Maggie. "Do you know if there are any more hot dogs?"

David tosses his shaggy bangs out of his eyes and grins. "Sure, there's one right there," he says, pointing to a Labrador retriever lying on the grass below.

I roll my eyes. David is always goofing around. Just about the only thing he's ever serious about is horses. They're his favorite animal, and he's a really good rider, even though he's only eleven, like Maggie and me.

"...and there's another one, and another one..." David continues to point out dogs.

"Never mind," Maggie mutters. "I'll go see for myself. Want one, Sunita?"

"Sure," I say.

David sits down on a bench. "It figures you'd find the one cat at the whole picnic, Sunita," he says. "You're like a cat magnet."

I smile but don't bother to answer. I'm still watching Lucy. Her eyes are half closed and she seems content now, but there's no hint of a purr.

Soon Maggie returns, holding two hot dogs— or, rather, one and a half hot dogs. She's already eaten half of hers. She pops the rest of it into her mouth and holds mine out to me. I blink at her, trying to figure out how to hold Lucy and eat the hot dog at the same time.

Maggie chews and swallows. "Here," she says. "I'll hold Lucy while you eat."

I hesitate. I'm still a little worried about Lucy. I wonder if she could be sick. Whenever an animal's behavior is different from usual, it could mean she's not feeling well. That's one of the first things that Dr. Mac taught us all when we started volunteering. Maybe I should mention this to her.

My stomach grumbles, and I decide the decision can wait a minute or two. "Okay," I say at last, handing Lucy over.

Maggie perches on the bench beside David,

settling Lucy on her lap. As I take a bite out of the hot dog, Brenna comes charging toward me leading Mercury, a huge black dog, along behind her. Brenna hardly ever walks at a normal pace. She has lots of energy, which comes in handy when there's work to do at the clinic. And there's always plenty of work to do at Dr. Mac's Place. That's why Dr. Mac invited the five of us—Maggie, Brenna, Zoe, David, and me—to volunteer here after school and in the summer.

Lucy sees Mercury and hisses at him, showing all her teeth. Her long, slender dark brown tail twitches, and her ears flatten back against her head.

"It's okay, Lucy." She leaps down from Maggie's lap and retreats behind my legs. I glance at Maggie and shrug. Lucy's not too crazy about big dogs. I don't blame her.

"Have you seen the dog biscuits?" Brenna asks breathlessly. Her long brown hair is escaping from its ponytail, and she looks just as hot as the rest of us. "I just taught Mercury how to sit up and beg, and I want to reward him."

"Good boy, Mercury!" David says, giving Mercury a quick scratch on the head.

I stand up and keep a cautious eye on Mercury.

He's awfully big—a rottweiler mix. I like dogs, but I prefer them on the smaller side. Mercury stares at my hot dog with his huge pink tongue hanging out of his mouth. I take a step backward.

Mercury takes a step toward me. He pulls his tongue into his mouth for a second, making a slurping sound. Then his jaw falls open again. He has an awful lot of teeth. I stare at him, hoping that Brenna has a tight hold on the leash.

David notices my expression and laughs at me. "Don't be so worried, scaredy-cat!" he says. "He just wants your hot dog."

"Um, I know." I keep my gaze on Mercury. What if he jumps at me and knocks me down?

"Brenna, I think Mrs. Creighton's terriers ate all the biscuits. Check inside for more," says Maggie.

"Thanks." Brenna takes off again, with Mercury trotting along behind her. Even with his long legs, the dog has to hurry to keep up.

I'm relieved to see them go. I sigh and put my hot dog down. I'm not really hungry anymore.

"What's up, Sunita?" Maggie asks, handing Lucy back to me.

"Nothing," I reply, cuddling Lucy.

Just then I see Dr. Mac heading toward the deck. A slim, well-dressed elderly woman with bluish-white hair is with her. "There you are, Sunita," Dr. Mac says when she reaches us.

"How are my girls?" Mrs. Clark says, giving me a friendly smile and her cat a rub under the chin. I love the way Mrs. Clark's greenish-brown eyes sparkle—it makes her look happy and wise and curious, all at the same time. "How's everything going? Is Lucy giving you any trouble?"

"Not exactly," I say, glancing from Dr. Mac to Mrs. Clark and back again. I quickly explain Lucy's odd behavior.

"That doesn't sound like her at all," Mrs. Clark agrees.

"Do you think we should check her glucose level?" I ask Dr. Mac.

"That's exactly what we should do, Sunita. Good call," she says. "Bring her on in."

Chapter Two

• • • • • • • • • • •

I follow Dr. Mac and Mrs. Clark into the Herriot Room and place Lucy on the exam table. I've helped Dr. Mac perform glucose tests on Lucy and other animals lots of times before. But right now I'm a little nervous. What if Lucy is having some kind of complication because of her diabetes? She is getting kind of old.

"All right, Lucy. Are you ready?" Dr. Mac says, and calmly approaches the Siamese with a needle.

I move forward and hold Lucy gently in place. Dr. Mac inserts the needle into a vein in Lucy's neck and draws the blood she'll need for the test. Lucy hardly moves.

"Brave girl," I say.

When she's finished drawing the blood, Dr. Mac gives Lucy a pat, then puts the blood sample into a centrifuge. That's a machine that separates the solid part of the blood—the red and white blood cells—from the fluid part. The clear-looking fluid is called serum, and it's the part that gets tested for its glucose level.

"When did she have her last meal, Esther?" Dr. Mac asks as she works.

"This morning at eight, as usual," Mrs. Clark replies. "She ate it all, like a good girl. She's been eating very well lately."

That's a good thing. In addition to giving her daily insulin injections, Mrs. Clark also has to be extra careful about what Lucy eats. She feeds her a special high-fiber, low-fat cat food in several small meals a day, instead of just leaving dry food down all the time like I do for Mittens. It's really important for diabetic cats to get regular meals as well as regular injections. Otherwise their sugar levels can get all messed up, and that can put their lives in danger.

I stroke the cat as Dr. Mac works. Lucy finally starts to purr, stretching out first her front and then her back legs so that her claws extend, then rolling onto her side and tilting her chin up for me to scratch. I smile, figuring that's all a good sign.

Sure enough, when Dr. Mac finishes with Lucy's tests, she tells Mrs. Clark, "Her sugar is fine."

"Oh, good," Mrs. Clark says with a smile. She picks up Lucy and hugs her. "Ready to go, sweetheart?"

"There are plenty of hot dogs left," I say, hoping Mrs. Clark will stay so I can hang out with Lucy a little longer.

"Thanks, but this damp weather isn't good for my old bones," Mrs. Clark says. "Or Lucy's, either. We're going to go home and try to stay dry."

Dr. Mac and I walk Mrs. Clark out to the reception area. Mrs. Clark settles her bill while Lucy sits on the counter, washing her face. Then Mrs. Clark picks up her cat. "Okay, girl," she says. "Let's get going before the storm gets any worse."

"You know how I feel about you driving with

Lucy, Esther," Dr. Mac says. "Why don't I lend you a cat carrier for the ride home?"

Mrs. Clark shakes her head firmly. "No, thank you. I've got a couple collecting dust in my attic. Lucy hates them. She'll be just fine riding on my lap, as usual."

Dr. Mac shrugs slightly, looking disappointed. She thinks all pets should be safely confined when they ride in a car. But she can't make her patients' owners do anything they don't want to do.

As I open the door for Mrs. Clark and say good-bye, I notice a van with a canoe tied on top of it parked in the lot next to the clinic. A customer named Mr. Jermaine—he always tells us to call him Bill—is standing nearby talking to David. He hurries to help Mrs. Clark climb into her car. Soon Mrs. Clark pulls away. I wave at Lucy, who is standing up and looking out the car window with her paws pressed against the glass.

Bill Jermaine walks over to me with a friendly smile on his face. "Hi there, Sunita," he says.

"Hi," I reply, tipping my head back to look up at him. He's a big man, tall and wide with a loud, booming voice. He makes David, who is right behind him, look even shorter and skinnier than he really is.

Bill Jermaine's wife, Jacqueline, climbs out of the van. She's just the opposite of her husband. She's petite, with dainty features and a soft, soothing voice. She's the weather reporter on one of the local TV stations. Bill Jermaine is a meteorologist, too—that's a scientist who studies the weather—but he teaches at the university.

"Hello, dear," Jacqueline says as I greet her politely. She calls everyone at the clinic "dear" except Dr. Mac. I don't think she remembers our names. She even calls Dr. Gabe "dear."

"Are you here for the picnic?" I ask as the sky releases a low rumble of thunder.

"Picnic?" Jacqueline says blankly. "No, we're just on our way home. We were supposed to go camping in the Poconos this weekend, but we both got called back to our offices. It seems that Felix is changing direction again." She sounds just like she does during her nightly weather reports on TV. "It looks like it's going to be moving farther up the coast instead of making landfall in the Carolinas."

"Farther up the coast?" I repeat. The idea of a hurricane coming our way is kind of scary.

"Whoa!" David says. "You mean, the hurricane is coming toward us?"

"Right," Bill says. "They're tracking it carefully, and it seems it won't make landfall until somewhere near Virginia or maybe farther north. That means our weather here in Pennsylvania will get a lot worse before it gets better. We're expecting bands of heavy rain for the next two to three days. And that's the forecast, whether you like it or not." He grins. His wife ends all of her reports on the news by saying that.

"So why are you here?" David asks.

"It's Stormy," Jacqueline says, opening the van door. "He's been acting weird the whole way home. I was hoping Dr. Mac could take a look at him."

I gulp as a huge black-and-white dog carefully climbs down from the van. Every time I see Stormy, I'm surprised all over again at how enormous he is. He's a Great Dane—that's one of the largest breeds of dog there is. Stormy is Dr. Mac's Place's largest patient with paws.

I smile nervously at Stormy, but he doesn't

seem to notice me. He sits down, tucks his tail between his legs, leans against the side of the van, and whines. He looks terrified.

"Hey! Stormy, old buddy!" David squats down beside the big dog, rubbing his chest. David's crazy about Stormy. I think it's because Stormy is almost as big as a horse!

The Great Dane wags his tail weakly when David pats him, then whines again and cringes against him. Jacqueline kneels beside her dog, looking worried. Before I can ask what's wrong with him, Dr. Mac appears at the clinic door. "Oh, hi, Jacqui and Bill," she greets the Jermaines with a smile. "Can't you do something about this weather? It's ruining my picnic," she jokes.

The Jermaines chuckle, then tell Dr. Mac about Stormy's behavior. He's still cringing against the van, looking miserable, even though David is petting and scratching him in all his favorite spots.

"Stormy's always a little nervous before a storm," Bill explains. "But not this bad. We want to make sure that's all there is to it."

"Poor guy. He looks like a dog, but he's really just a big scaredy-cat." David grins up at me. I feel my cheeks turn red. David doesn't know how to let something drop. I hope he's not going to start calling me scaredy-cat all the time.

Dr. Mac gazes at Stormy thoughtfully. "Why don't you bring him in?" she suggests. "I can take a quick look."

"Could you?" Jacqueline looks relieved. "Thank you so much. That would make us feel a lot better." She puts one hand over her heart. Everything she does is dramatic. I guess that comes from being on TV every day.

I follow Dr. Mac, David, and the Jermaines inside, making sure there's plenty of room between me and Stormy. He looks even more enormous once we're all in the reception area. I know he's a gentle, well-behaved, friendly dog that wouldn't hurt a flea. But that doesn't stop me from being a little uneasy around him.

Dr. Mac is staring at him, her eyes thoughtful and distant, the way they always get when she's concentrating on something. "Sunita, could you help me with the exam, please?"

"Me?" I gulp, glancing at Stormy out of the corner of my eye. "Sure, I—"

"I'll do it," David interrupts. He steps up and gives Stormy another pat. "It'll take a strong kid like me to help keep Stormy on the exam table.

Besides, Stormy likes my Scooby-Doo imita-
tion."

I force a smile as he follows Dr. Mac, Stormy,
and Jacqueline into the Dolittle Room. But I have
a queasy sort of feeling in the pit of my stomach.
I sink down onto one of the chairs in the reception area. *Am I really a scaredy-cat?*

Chapter Three

. . . .

Do you mind if I sit here with you, Sunita?" Bill Jermaine says. "That exam room is too small for both Stormy and me, and I don't want to get in the doctor's way."

I glance at him, suddenly realizing that he hasn't followed the others. "No problem," I say weakly, forcing another smile. I don't want him to see that I'm upset. I especially don't want him to guess that his big dog scares me, at least a little. It wouldn't look good for someone who volunteers at a vet clinic.

"Thanks," Bill says, sitting down beside me. The chair squeaks a little under his weight.

At that moment Socrates, Dr. Mac's cat, wanders into the room. He stops and looks at us for a moment. I'm expecting him to come to me, but he goes to Bill instead. With a small meow, he butts his big orange head against Bill's shin.

"That's strange," Bill says, raising one eyebrow as he leans over to pat Socrates gingerly on the back. "This cat never gave me the time of day before."

It's more than strange. Socrates isn't the friendly type, like Lucy. He's more of a look-but-don't-touch kind of cat. Just about the only people he lets pet him are Dr. Mac and me.

"He's acting like a completely different cat," I comment as Socrates weaves in and out around Bill's legs. "I wonder if there's something wrong with him."

"I wouldn't worry too much," Bill says. "It's probably Hurricane Felix that's affecting him, just like Stormy."

"The hurricane?" I say. "What do you mean? Does Stormy know that it's coming this way?"

"Well, he probably wouldn't put it so specifically. But yes, he knows something is wacky about the weather—like now, he knows a big storm is brewing. Animals are good at sensing that."

"Are you saying that animals can predict the weather before it happens?" I ask.

"Not exactly." Bill smiles. "They use their five regular senses just like us, only they're a little more perceptive than we are about certain environmental changes, like air pressure and static electricity. As a cat lover, you might notice that static electricity in the air often makes cats groom themselves more."

"That explains why Lucy was acting so weird today," I say. When Bill stares at me blankly, I add, "Mrs. Clark's cat. And she was grooming herself a lot, too."

Bill nods. "It's not just cats and dogs who react to the weather," he says. "Falling or changing air pressure can cause deer and other animals to come down from the mountains and look for shelter. Swallows fly lower. Cows lie down a lot more. Even mosquitoes and other flying insects get more active and stay closer to the ground."

I nod my head thoughtfully. What Bill is saying makes me think of something I learned in school last year. "My science teacher taught us how to count a cricket's chirps to tell how hot it is. You count the number of chirps in fourteen seconds, then add forty to that number to get the temperature."

"That's right." Bill grins. "It's actually pretty accurate most of the time. So you see, it's not just poor Stormy who reacts to weather changes. All sorts of animals, birds, and insects do. People, too." He glances at the exam-room door. "Stormy has always reacted strongly to that sort of thing. And this is the worst storm we've been through since we've had him. He's pretty stressed out."

Just then the door to the exam room opens, and Dr. Mac pokes her head out. "Oh, good, Sunita," she says when she sees me. "You're still here. I need your help.

I gulp and stand up. "What do you need me to do?" I ask Dr. Mac, trying to sound professional and not at all nervous as I head toward her.

Dr. Mac is scribbling something on a small pad of paper. She doesn't answer for a second. Then she finishes her writing and rips off the sheet. "Here," she says, handing it to me. "Could you please go back to the supply closet and find a bottle of these tranquilizers? I think they're on the second shelf to the right."

I stare at the piece of paper in my hand. Dr. Mac doesn't need my help with Stormy. She just wants me to run and fetch some medicine. "Of course," I say, relieved. "I'll be right back."

As I hurry out of the room, I can't help smiling a little about Stormy's problem. It seems funny that a meteorologist's dog named Stormy hates storms so much. It's also kind of weird to think about a huge dog like that being afraid of anything.

When I get back from the supply closet, the Jermaines are out in the reception area. Stormy is lying on the cool floor near the desk.

I hand the tranquilizer bottle to Dr. Mac. "Here," I say. "Will Stormy be all right?"

"Absolutely." Dr. Mac bends over to pat the big dog. "I gave him a dose in the exam room, and he's calmer already, as you can see. Most dogs with this kind of anxiety don't need any medication, but Stormy is an extreme case. It's safer to tranquilize a dog than to let him drive himself crazy with anxiety and possibly injure himself."

Bill glances at his watch. "Well, we'd better get going," he says. "We've got our work cut out for us these next couple of days."

Dr. Mac nods. "Drive carefully," she says, and

gives the Jermaines some last-minute instruc-
tions about the tranquilizers. When she opens
the door for them, a sheet of rain sweeps in,
splashing onto the floor halfway across the
room. A crack of thunder booms suddenly, making everyone jump.

"Wow." David whistles. "I guess the picnic is
over."

Sure enough, when we head outside, most
of the guests have already gone. The remain-
ing ones are hurrying toward their cars, holding jackets and newspapers and anything else
they can find over their heads. Maggie, Zoe, and
Brenna are rushing around trying to get everything out of the rain.

"Look on the bright side, though," David adds.
"At least we're not broiling anymore."

He's right. I realize the air has turned a little
chilly. A shiver runs down my arms.

Dr. Mac sighs. "Come on," she says. "Let's go
help the girls clean up before this whole place
floats away."

An hour later, Zoe pulls up the shade on the

waiting-room window. "It's raining really, really hard now," she reports.

"That's what you've been saying for the past half hour," Maggie snaps.

Zoe wrinkles her nose. "No, I haven't," she retorts. "The last few times I said it was raining really hard. Now it's raining really, *really* hard."

"Whatever," Maggie mutters. "You still sound like a broken record." Even though Maggie and Zoe are cousins, they don't always get along too well. Actually, they're practically opposites. Ever since Zoe moved to Ambler from New York City, Maggie has been getting on her case about how she loves to shop and do other girlie stuff. Zoe likes to tease Maggie about her sloppy clothes and the way she's so into sports. Besides that, the triple-H weather seems to be making everyone a little crabby.

A gust of wind rattles the windows, and I look up from the patient files I'm updating. "I wonder how close Hurricane Felix is by now," I say.

Any possible response is drowned out by a loud howl from the direction of Dr. Mac's house, which is attached to the clinic. David winces and looks up from sweeping the floor under the guest chairs. "Poor Sherlock," he says. "He sounds like he's being tortured."

Sherlock has been whining and howling off and on for the past hour. Every time there's a clap of thunder or an especially violent gust of wind, he starts up again. Even though he's in the house, on the other side of the wall from the clinic, the noise is giving me a headache. Basset hounds can be loud—and I mean loud. Besides, each time he howls, most of the dogs back in the kennel area join in with their own barking and wailing.

"Sherlock sure will be glad when this storm is over," Maggie says.

"So will Stormy," David adds.

So will I.

Brenna is looking out the window now. "Wow," she says. "There's like a little river running through the front yard."

"Cool. If we get flooded in, I can paddle us out. I was canoe champion at day camp last year," David brags.

Maggie rolls her eyes. "Oh, please," she says. "I could beat you with one paddle tied behind my back."

"Yeah, right." David lets out a loud, sarcastic snort. "You wish!"

I sigh. Maggie and David are always arguing about stuff like that. Usually it's kind of funny— like the time they had an arm-wrestling contest, and both of them refused to give in until Brenna and Zoe and I started tickling them. But today I'm not in the mood to listen to them bicker.

"Has anyone fed the boarders yet?" I ask, glancing at my watch. "Dr. Mac wanted us to get that done before four o'clock."

"Nope," Brenna replies. "Not me."

The others shake their heads. I glance at the files in my lap. "Well?" I say. "Is anyone going to do it?"

"I thought you were volunteering, Sunita," Zoe says. She's sitting in one of the visitors' chairs picking aqua nail polish off her big toe. Sneakers, her mutt, is obediently sitting beside her. He's a great dog now that he's housebroken.

I glare at her. "I'm busy right now," I snap.

Zoe rolls her eyes. "If you want me to do it, just say so," she says. "Come on, Brenna. Want to help me?"

I frown as the two of them leave the room.

For a few minutes, it's silent in the reception area. Maggie is bent over her work, and even David doesn't seem to feel like talking for a change. Sherlock stops howling—for a moment, at least. I sigh.

Suddenly the front door bursts open, letting in another squall of wind and rain. I'm startled to see Mrs. Clark rushing in. She has a towel-wrapped bundle in her arms.

"Help!" she cries. "Lucy's hurt!"

Chapter Four

. . . .

Lucy looks awful. Her fur is matted from the rain. Her eyes are huge and scared. The lower part of her left front leg is swollen right above her paw. Her mouth is open slightly, and she's panting sort of like a dog. That means she's in shock from the pain. She lets out a pitiful meow and tries to lift her head.

Dr. Mac hurries out of her office. "What happened?" she asks as she carefully takes Lucy from Mrs. Clark.

"Lucy and I had just arrived home," Mrs. Clark responds breathlessly, water dripping down her face from her wet hair. "We had stopped off to visit a friend on our way back from the picnic, and the wind and rain were awful by then, so I decided to carry her instead of letting her walk."

Dr. Mac nods. I figure she's probably thinking that Mrs. Clark should have used the cat carrier she offered her, but she doesn't say so.

"We were almost to the front door when there was a big clap of thunder," Mrs. Clark goes on. "Lucy and I were both startled. She jumped out of my arms in a panic, and she hit the door pretty hard."

I wince. Poor Lucy! But there's no time to think about that. Dr. Mac is already heading for the Herriot Room.

This time I follow her.

"Maggie, we need to anesthetize and X-ray. David, why don't you get out the splinting equipment in case there is a fracture. Sunita, come over here and stand by Lucy. Watch her carefully for any signs of distress."

I nod and move quickly into place. "It's okay, sweetie," I croon to Lucy as soothingly as I can. I wish I could pet her to let her know everything will be okay, but I know I shouldn't. "Just stay still now. We know it hurts, but we're here to help."

Meanwhile Dr. Mac examines Lucy, checking her vital signs gently but quickly. She looks at the cat's gums. I see a flash of pale pink.

"She's in mild shock—not too bad," Dr. Mac says. "We'd better get a little oxygen into her and start her on some IV fluids. Then we'll give her an anesthetic so I can take a closer look at her leg."

Dr. Mac puts an oxygen mask over Lucy's face. I hold it there while she inserts the IV catheter and starts the fluids. Then she moves away to help Maggie prepare the anesthetic.

"Hang in there, Lucy," I murmur, trying to look into the cat's eyes. I want her to know that I'm here and that Dr. Mac is going to make her feel better very soon. I glance across the room at Mrs. Clark, who is being careful to stay out of the way. The elderly woman's face is pale and scared. I wish I could reassure her that Lucy is going to be all right, but I know Mrs. Clark won't feel better until this is all over. So I don't say anything. I return my attention to Lucy, hoping she can feel the good thoughts I'm sending her.

Dr. Mac returns with a syringe. "Okay," she says, "this will make you feel better, girl." She injects the anesthetic with one smooth move.

I watch Lucy's eyelids droop lower and lower until she's unconscious. Her breathing has slowed, and she looks relaxed. Dr. Mac carefully carries Lucy into the X-ray room. I follow her so that I can keep watch while the X-ray is being taken.

A couple of minutes later, Dr. Mac, Lucy, and I are back in the Herriot Room. Dr. Mac sticks the X-ray film on the light box on the wall and flips a switch to turn it on. "Hmm," she says. "It's broken, all right."

Dr. Mac points out a section of the image to Mrs. Clark. "Luckily, it's a closed fracture, so it shouldn't be too hard to take care of."

I exchange a relieved glance with Maggie and David. I've been at the clinic long enough to know that a closed fracture is when a broken bone hasn't broken through the skin. When it does, it's called a compound fracture and it's a little trickier, since the wound could get infected. Because of Lucy's diabetes, infections can be especially dangerous.

"Will she be all right?" Mrs. Clark asks in a quivering voice. "We've been together so long,

I couldn't stand it if she..." She stops, seeming afraid to finish the sentence.

Dr. Mac flashes her a smile. "She'll be fine," she assures her. "It's a hairline fracture, and it's in the lower part of the leg where it's easier to set. With a little luck, she'll be as good as new once it heals."

Mrs. Clark looks relieved. David has already heated a pan of water on a special hot plate. Now Dr. Mac picks up a sheet of bright blue plastic. She dips the thin plastic sheet into the warm water, letting it soften.

"What's that?" Mrs. Clark asks nervously.

"It's the splint," Dr. Mac explains as she pulls the now pliable plastic out of the water. "I was just softening it so that I can shape it around Lucy's broken leg. The fit will be nice and snug once it cools and hardens up again."

Dr. Mac works quickly, fitting the warm plastic around Lucy's foreleg. I wish I could do more to help, but Dr. Mac has everything under control. She finishes shaping the plastic splint, then steps back so we can all see it. "Would you bring me some bandages, Maggie, please?" she asks. After she carefully wraps the splint with the bandages, she steps back again, looking satisfied. "All finished," she says. "Now all we have to do is let her wake up."

Maggie steps forward. "Would you like a cup of tea or something while you wait?" she asks Mrs. Clark.

"Oh, a cup of tea would be nice." Mrs. Clark smiles at Maggie gratefully. "Thank you. Lemon, no sugar, please."

"Okay. I'll be right back." Maggie hurries out of the room.

David and I start cleaning up the exam room while Dr. Mac and Mrs. Clark talk about the storm. It doesn't take long for Lucy to come around. First the cat's long tail starts twitching, then she tries to lift her head. It wobbles weakly, and she lets out a soft meow. Mrs. Clark gently pets her.

"Don't worry, Lucy," she croons. "The doctor made you all better. Now we can go home."

"Why don't you let her stay until she's fully awake," Dr. Mac suggests. "I can check her glucose level before she goes home."

"All right." Mrs. Clark seems relieved to see her cat stirring again.

A few minutes later, Maggie returns, carefully

carrying a mug with a picture of a schnauzer on it. Dr. Mac has a whole collection of animal mugs—her patients' owners like to give them to her for Christmas. Mrs. Clark takes the tea and sips it gently.

"When should I bring her in next?" she asks Dr. Mac as Lucy sniffs weakly at the strange contraption on her leg.

"I'd like to see Lucy once a week until this is healed," Dr. Mac says. "I'll need to change the bandage and check the fracture site. In the meantime, call if there are any problems or if you notice swelling. But knowing Lucy, I'm sure she won't let a little thing like a broken leg keep her down for long. Do your best to keep her as quiet as possible while she heals." She smiles and reaches over to scratch the woozy cat behind her ears. "She'll be groggy for a couple of hours, but she should come out of it just fine."

Mrs. Clark bites her lip as she watches Lucy try to sit up. The cat wobbles and tips over. "Are you sure she'll be all right?"

I can tell she's worried. Lucy looks pretty awful right now. "I could stop by in the morning and check on her if you'd like," I offer, looking from Dr. Mac to Mrs. Clark. "Just to make sure she's doing well."

"Oh, that would be wonderful, Sunita," Mrs. Clark says gratefully. "I'm sure it will make Lucy feel better to have a visit from her favorite young girl."

I'm pleased that Mrs. Clark thinks of me that way. "Okay, then," I say. "I'll come over on my way to the clinic tomorrow."

"Good." Dr. Mac nods her approval. "Esther, this may affect Lucy's insulin level, so you should monitor her carefully for a few days. Make sure she's eating and drinking the same amount as usual."

Mrs. Clark nods. "Thank you," she tells Dr. Mac. "I'm just so relieved that she's going to be okay. I don't know what I'd do without her."

By the time Mrs. Clark finishes her tea, Lucy is more alert. Dr. Mac checks over the cat once more, then says it's all right for them to leave. "We'll send her home in this," Dr. Mac adds, pulling out a lightweight plastic cat carrier from the cabinet under the sink.

This time, Mrs. Clark accepts it without protest. Soon Lucy is settled inside on a clean towel.

Before latching the wire door, I reach inside and scratch Lucy in her favorite spot under her chin, being careful not to disturb the splint on her leg. "You'll be fine, Lucy," I whisper as I lift the carrier. "Just rest now. I'll see you tomorrow."

"Good-bye, everyone," Mrs. Clark calls as she heads toward the door. "And thank you so much for everything." I slip into my raincoat and then follow with the cat carrier.

It takes only a few minutes to put the carrier into Mrs. Clark's car and say good-bye to her and Lucy. But by the time I return to the clinic, I'm soaked to the skin. "Whew!" I exclaim as I lower the hood on my raincoat. "It's like a monsoon out there."

"I think you kids had better head home before the storm gets any worse," Dr. Mac says, checking her watch. "I doubt we'll have any more patients today."

"Roger." David is already reaching for his raincoat, which is hanging near the door. "See you tomorrow."

"Maybe." Dr. Mac glances at the rain pounding against the window. "If the weather is too bad in the morning, don't try to come in. Maggie

and Zoe and I can hold down the fort if necessary. Okay?"

I nod along with David. But I know that I have
to brave Hurricane Felix the next day, no matter
how bad it is. Lucy is counting on me.

Chapter Five

. . . .

When I get home a few minutes later, I let myself in the back door and breathe in the delicious smell of Mother's famous chicken tandoori. It makes me feel a little warmer, even though I'm drenched. I hang my raincoat on the hook near the garage door and walk over to the sink. That's strange. Where's Mittens? She's usually the first to greet me.

As I'm doing my best to squeeze most of the water out of my long, thick hair, my mother comes into the kitchen.

"Sunita, Mittens is acting crazy," Mother says, her dark brown eyes anxious. "She's howling like a wildcat, and she won't come out from under your bed."

That doesn't sound like Mittens at all. "I hope she's not sick," I say, heading toward the stairs.

I race up to my bedroom and flop down on the floor. Lifting the lace bedskirt, I peer into the dark space beneath my bed. A pair of glowing eyes greets me from the farthest corner by the wall.

"Waaah-oooh!"

The noise Mittens makes doesn't even sound like a cat. It's more like the howl of some creature from another planet.

"Here, kitty kitty," I croon, scooting forward a little more with the help of the hooked rug by my bed. "Come on out, Mittens. Please?"

Mittens howls again. As my eyes adjust to the dark, I can see that her ears are pricked toward me. Obviously she hears me—but she still isn't coming out. After a moment, she creeps forward a little bit and meows uncertainly. Her black-and-white fur is fluffed up, and her tail twitches nervously.

"Come on, pretty girl," I coax her. "That's right. Come on out."

It takes a while, but finally I get her to come

close enough for me to grab her. I pull her out as carefully as I can, hoping that she's not injured or sick. *Please just let it be the weather, like Mr. Jermaine says.* I carry her into the bathroom across the hall and shut the door so that she can't get away from me. Now there are fewer places for her to hide.

As soon as I put her down, she crouches low. There's a distant boom of thunder. It's not very loud, but Mittens jerks her head around nervously, yowls, then leaps straight into the air, almost knocking over the white wicker towel caddy as she races over to wedge herself behind the toilet. Black fur floats in the air behind her. She's shedding like crazy. That's what most cats do when they're nervous.

I sigh. "I don't think you're sick, sweetie," I say, leaning back against the whitewashed vanity cabinet. "It's just Hurricane Felix. You should be glad you aren't Lucy. Not only is she weirded out by the weather like you are, but she has a broken leg, too."

Thoughts about Lucy distract me. She must really have been scared to jump out of Mrs. Clark's arms like that. I hope she eats all her food tonight.

Mittens lets out another yowl, which brings me back to the here and now. My poor kitty's peering out from her hiding place, looking terrified. From what I can see out the bathroom window, I can't really blame her. The sky is dark and ominous, and rain is slashing against the glass as if it's trying to break in.

I talk to Mittens for a few more minutes, trying to comfort her. But she doesn't even seem to hear me. We'll have to wait for the storm to pass. I wonder how long that'll be? I decide to check the Internet.

Figuring that Mittens will probably feel safest in her original hiding spot, I let her out of the bathroom. Sure enough, she races straight for my room and darts under the bed again.

• • • • • • •

"Well?" Mother asks when I go back downstairs. "Did you see her?"

"Uh-huh. I think she wants to be alone right now. She's just scared of Hurricane Felix," I explain. "Is it all right if I turn on the computer? I want to see how much longer this storm will last."

"All right," she says. "But if that lightning gets any closer, turn it off right way."

I nod and head into the den. As soon as I get online, I check the weather site we have bookmarked. The satellite image shows one band of rain clouds after another, with the storm's eye hovering around the coast of Virginia. Then I type the word *hurricane* into a search engine. About a zillion sites come up. "Hmm," I murmur, scanning the first few on the list. "Guess I should be more specific."

This time I type the words *hurricane* and *pets*. Soon I'm skimming an article about getting your pets safely through a weather emergency. It says that every family should have a plan of action before disaster strikes.

"It's a little late for that," I mutter, glancing at the rain pounding against the window.

I read a little further. Uh-oh. The site says that Red Cross emergency shelters can't take in animals, except for service dogs such as guide dogs for the blind. That can't be right. I hit the "back" button to return to my search results and check another page. But it says the same thing. In fact, it notes that most human emergency shelters of any kind won't let people bring their pets.

I guess that's why it's so important to plan ahead. I wonder how many people in Ambler have made plans for their pets in case there's flooding from all the rain. Probably not many. We don't have too many natural disasters here.

I don't realize Mother is standing behind me until she clears her throat. "You'd better turn off the computer now, Sunita," she says. "The lightning is getting closer, and we could lose power at any moment."

"Mom, do we have an emergency plan?" I ask.

She looks at the site I'm reading. "We have a fire escape plan," she says. "But don't worry. I'm sure we'll be fine here."

I quickly scan the rest of the site. "But it says here that inland flooding is one of the deadliest parts of a hurricane, even if the winds aren't that strong," I tell Mother. "The heavy rains and flooding can affect people hundreds of miles from the ocean. See?" I point to the paragraph I'm reading. "It says here that Hurricane Floyd killed fifty-six people when it hit the eastern U.S. in 1999. And out of those fifty-six people, fifty drowned due to inland flooding."

"Yes, flooding can be very dangerous. But our house is built on high ground." Mother puts a hand on my shoulder as thunder rumbles again. "Don't worry, Sunita," she adds with a little squeeze. "Please turn off the computer now. I need you to help me check the downstairs windows to make sure they're all closed. That'll be the first part of our plan."

I do as she says. As we walk from room to room checking the windows, I'm still thinking about what I just read. I guess Mother is thinking about the hurricane, too, because neither of us says much.

"I hope your father gets home from the hospital soon," Mother comments as we check the living room.

We stand together staring out the front window. There's so much rain that I can hardly see to the end of the driveway. "Me, too," I agree.

Mother hardly seems to hear me. A little furrow creases her brow. "The roads must be terrible. Sunita, could you check the upstairs windows? I want to bring my cell phone in from the car in case our regular phones go out."

"Sure." I head upstairs. My little brother and sister are playing in the hall, racing some toy cars up and down on the smooth floorboards. They look up when they see me.

"Sunita, your hair is wet!" Jasmine exclaims. "Did you take a bath?"

"No," I tell her, running a hand over my damp hair. It's so thick that it takes forever to dry. "I was outside in the storm. It's really raining hard."

Harshil nods, looking excited. "It's a hurricane," he tells me. "Daddy says that's a really, really big storm. Daddy says the storm's name is Feligs."

"That's Felix," I say, smiling. "With an *X*."

"Maybe we should go see if our yard is flooded yet," Jasmine says, looking worried.

"Yeah!" Harshil jumps to his feet. "If our house floods, will all our toys float away?"

"No, of course not. We don't have to worry," says a reassuring voice behind me.

I turn around. It's Daddy. "I'm so glad you're home." I sigh, and smile.

The twins run to hug his legs.

He rubs their heads and says, "Our neighborhood is on pretty high ground. Most of this part of town is. The only ones who need to worry are the people over in the Oakwood area, outside of town." Then he adds, "Oh, and maybe houses down on Willow Street. One of my patients lives in one of those old homes down there, and they got flooded out about ten years ago."

For a second I'm so relieved to hear that our house is safe that I don't take in what my father just said. Then I gasp. Willow Street? That's where Mrs. Clark and Lucy live!

Chapter Six

. . . .

Whoa," I mutter, grabbing the front door against a heavy gust of wind. The sky still looks gray and gloomy this morning. It's been raining all night, but right now it's only drizzling lightly. I saw on TV that Felix made landfall a couple of hours ago in southern New Jersey. I'd really hate to see what the wind is like down there.

I glance over my shoulder at the cozy, dry living room behind me. For half a second I'm tempted to close the door and stay inside. Dr. Mac can manage without me. But then I remember Lucy. I have to check on her. It seems even more important now because of the storm. What if there has been some problem with Lucy's splint or complications because of her diabetes, and Mrs. Clark can't get to the clinic because of Hurricane Felix?

Mother appears behind me, peering out at the steel-gray clouds. "Sunita, maybe you should stay home today. I'm not sure you should be wandering around town in this weather."

"It's only a few blocks to Mrs. Clark's house, and then I'll go straight to the clinic. Besides, it's hardly raining anymore." I hold my breath, hoping Mother won't remember that Mrs. Clark lives on Willow Street. If she remembers that and thinks there might be any flooding, she might not let me go.

Mother still looks uncertain, but finally she nods. "All right," she says. "But be careful. Call me at the hospital when you get there."

"I will." I smile at her as reassuringly as I can. It's amazing. When I first started volunteering at the clinic almost six months ago, my parents hardly ever let me do anything on my own. I think working with Dr. Mac might have convinced them that I can handle more responsibility than they thought. And if Mother can make it to work today, so can I.

I brace myself and head out the door. As I cross the street and walk down the block, it starts to rain harder. Then a gust of wind whips the hood of my raincoat right off my head. "Ugh," I say, grabbing it and squinting against the rain blowing into my eyes. There's no traffic in sight—unless you count the empty trash can spinning crazily down the street toward me. I jump aside to avoid it.

Lucy needs me. Lucy needs me. I repeat the thought over and over, timing the words to my steps. It helps to keep me going as I trudge toward Willow Street. I don't pass a single pedestrian, and only a few cars go by, their tires throwing up sheets of water from the puddles on the road. Quite a lot of tree branches blew down overnight, and leaves and stray bits of paper are blowing around everywhere.

Finally I reach Willow Street. The little patch of grass in front of Mrs. Clark's old-fashioned one-story brick house is submerged under a giant puddle. The water looks deep enough to slosh over the edges of my boots, but I try not to think about it.

Mrs. Clark opens the door before I can knock.

"Sunita!" she says, looking happy to see me. "I wasn't sure you'd make it."

"Here I am," I reply. "How's Lucy? Is her splint okay? Is she eating normally? The storm isn't bothering her too much, is it?"

Mrs. Clark chuckles. "J.J. is training you well, Sunita," she says. "You're starting to sound just like her."

I blush. "So Lucy's all right?"

"She's just fine. But why don't you come on in, dry off, and see for yourself." Mrs. Clark gestures around her. "Sorry it's a bit stuffy. The wind was gusting so much that I had to close all the windows."

I follow Mrs. Clark down a narrow hallway toward the kitchen at the back of the house. "Whew!" I say as I carefully unzip my raincoat, trying not to get myself or Mrs. Clark's kitchen floor any wetter. "What a storm."

Mrs. Clark waves one hand dismissively. "This?" she says. "This is nothing. Why, in my day we wouldn't have even bothered to bring in the laundry for a little rainstorm like this."

I suspect that she's exaggerating, but I don't say so. It feels safe and warm inside the cozy kitchen. Mrs. Clark's house is pretty old, and the walls creak and groan as the wind attacks from outside. But the sound of the rain is muffled as it whips against the window above the sink. "It looks like your yard is flooded," I say.

"Oh, that happens every time there's a light shower." Mrs. Clark doesn't seem worried at all. "It's just poor drainage. Nothing to panic about."

Just then Lucy wanders into the room, moving pretty well despite her splint. "Mrrwowrr!" she greets me cheerfully.

"Lucy!" I kneel down on the floor to say hello. "You look just like your old self again. Well, almost."

"She's a tough cookie." Mrs. Clark smiles fondly at her cat. "She's getting around fine— everywhere but on the stairs. That reminds me. I wonder if you could do me a favor?"

"Sure," I say. "What is it?"

"Lucy's litter box is in the basement, but she's not too good at the stairs with that cast on." Mrs. Clark waves at a door across the room. "I tried to bring it up, but it's too heavy for my bad back. Could you get it for me?"

"No problem." I stand up and head for the basement door. "I'll get it right now."

The basement steps are quite steep, so I'm extra glad now that I braved the hurricane and came over. Otherwise Lucy could have ended up with a second broken leg!

The light in the basement is pretty dim, but I've been down there before to change the kitty litter while cat-sitting. I head straight for the litter box. Splash! My foot lands in a puddle.

"Yikes," I murmur, peering down. I notice that there are several shallow puddles on the concrete floor. My heart starts pounding faster as I remember what my parents said about Willow Street.

I hoist the litter box in both arms. It's heavy and kind of smelly, but I just hold my breath and move as fast as I can. Maybe I'm not such a wimp after all.

When I reach the kitchen, I set the box in the corner where Mrs. Clark directs me. As soon as it's in place, Lucy comes over to sniff at it. She wants to make sure it's hers.

I tell Mrs. Clark about the puddles in the basement. "Maybe you and Lucy should think about going to stay with friends or something," I suggest. "Just until the storm passes."

"Nonsense." Mrs. Clark chuckles. "A little water in the basement doesn't mean a thing. Besides, I rode out many a hurricane in my day back in South Carolina. A lot bigger ones than this, too. Lucy and I will be fine right here at home."

I bite my lip. For a second I'm tempted to argue. But I remember how Mrs. Clark despised using a cat carrier until yesterday. If Dr. Mac couldn't change Mrs. Clark's mind about something like that, what chance do I have to convince her about this? Besides, she's been through lots of hurricanes. This is my first one. What do I know? I'm probably worrying too much.

From Mrs. Clark's kitchen window, I see that the sky is even darker than it was when I came in. "I'd better get going," I say. "Dr. Mac probably needs my help at the clinic."

"All right, dear. Thank you for stopping by." Mrs. Clark picks up Lucy, and the two of them walk me to the door.

I plunge out into the rain, which seems to be coming down harder than when I left the house this morning. The wind takes my breath away at first, and I have to squint to see as the rain stings my face. I pause, wondering if I should just head home. Dr. Mac told David and me that we shouldn't come in if the weather was too bad. David . . . he'll think I'm a scaredy-cat if I don't show up.

The clinic is just a few blocks away. I cross Mrs. Clark's yard with my head down against the wind, but I catch a glimpse of that puddle in the corner of the yard as I pass by. Is it a little bigger than when I got there? Or is it just my imagination? There's no way to be sure.

· · · · · · ·

I'm still thinking about that puddle in the yard—and the ones in the basement—when I get back to the clinic. The phone is ringing when I walk in. There's nobody else in the reception area, so I throw my body against the door to push it closed against the howling wind, then rush over to pick up the phone.

"Hello, Dr. Mac's Place," I say. "Can I help you?"

"It's an emergency!" a breathless, panicky voice answers. "My little Precious girl won't eat her food and she keeps shivering, and a tree fell over so I can't get the car out of my driveway to bring her in, and I just know she's sick—"

"Um, hold on a second, please," I interrupt. "I'll get Dr. Mac."

I've already recognized the woman's voice. I hurry back to the recovery room, where I find Dr. Mac changing the gauze bandage on a corgi with a torn toenail. "It's Mrs. Creighton," I tell her. "She says Precious is shivering and not eating, and she can't get her car out of the driveway to come over." Mrs. Creighton is one of our most frequent visitors to the clinic. She has two tiny Yorkshire terriers, and she gets hysterical if one of them sneezes or coughs or looks at her funny.

Dr. Mac sighs. "Oh, dear," she says, looking harried. "Precious is probably just anxious because of the weather. But she's so nervous, even missing a meal or two could stress her enough to upset her stomach again. I suppose I'd better get over there and check on her. She may need a dextrose injection."

I help her return the corgi to his cage. Then, as Dr. Mac hurries toward the phone, I wander into the kennel area, where the other volunteers are doing chores.

When I tell them about the phone call, Zoe rolls her eyes. "Mrs. Creighton is a nut," she comments. "Precious is probably on a hunger strike to try to get herself a new owner."

I expect Maggie to argue with her—maybe launch into some long speech about dextrose injections. But she just nods. "Mrs. Creighton worries too much," she says. "And those little dogs know it, so they walk all over her. Precious probably decided she doesn't like her brand of dog food."

As Maggie talks, she's letting a dog I've never seen before out of one of the wire kennels. He looks like a small collie or sheltie mix. "Who's that?" I ask.

"His name's Otis." Brenna reaches down to scratch the dog behind the ears. "Someone found him wandering around and brought him here for safekeeping."

Maggie nods. "Dr. Mac called his owners—the number's on his tags—but their phone doesn't seem to be working, probably because of good old Felix. She's keeping an eye on him here until we can get in touch with them."

"Good thing he's wearing his tags." I watch the little dog cheerfully follow Maggie toward the back door. It would be terrible to lose your pet in a storm and not know how to find him. It makes me glad that Mittens is safe and sound inside my house.

I wander back toward the front. Dr. Mac is just hanging up the phone. She pulls on her raincoat and grabs her keys from the desk. "Dr. Gabe just called to say he was leaving the Jenkins farm—their llama decided she just had to give birth during this hurricane. He should be back shortly."

"Okay," I say. I can't help but feel a twinge of worry. What if we have a real emergency while both vets are out?

I don't think about that for long. There are chores to do. The first hour passes quickly. We clean the exam rooms, wash and refill the water dishes in all the occupied kennel cages, and bring the files and calendar up to date. Then we start to run out of things to do. The five of us keep as busy as we can doing whatever we can think of to do. By the time another half hour passes, the entire clinic is spotless. Every surface and piece of equipment shines. Every item, from penicillin to paper clip, is stowed in its proper place. Every dog has been fed, and all the kenneled cats have clean, fresh litter boxes.

I'm in the reception area thinking about calling Mom at the hospital when the phone rings. I cross my fingers and check my watch as I pick it up. Dr. Mac left almost an hour ago, but Mrs. Creighton and Precious live all the way across town. Maybe Dr. Mac is calling to say that she's on her way back. "Hello?" I say. "Dr. Mac's Place."

"Hi, Sunita," a familiar voice responds. "It's Dr. Gabe."

"Dr. Gabe!" I exclaim. "Where are you? Dr. Mac thought you'd be back here by now."

He laughs. "So did I. But Hurricane Felix had other ideas. The wind knocked down an oak tree on the road right in front of the Jenkins farm, and it's blocking my path. They're hooking a truck up to it to pull it out of the way, but it could be a while."

He sounds tired. "So you'll be back as soon as that's done?" I ask.

"I hope so," Dr. Gabe replies. "But it's been raining pretty hard since I got here, and a lot of the roads were starting to flood even on my way over. I just hope I can find a way around the worst spots. How are things at the clinic?"

"Fine." I don't tell him that Dr. Mac is out. There's nothing he can do about it anyway, and it might make him worry. "Really quiet, actually."

"Good. Let J.J. know I'll be there when I can."

"I will." *As soon as she gets back,* I add silently. "Drive carefully."

"Thanks. Stay dry, Sunita!"

"Okay. Bye." As I hang up the phone, I bite my lip and glance at my watch, wondering when Dr. Mac will be back.

"Who was that?" Maggie asks.

I tell her about Dr. Gabe's problem. "He's not sure when he'll be able to get through."

"Figures," Maggie says with a grimace. "Well, we'd better just hope that—"

Zoe rushes in, interrupting. "I just saw a news report on TV," she reports breathlessly. "They've started evacuating part of town because of major flooding!"

Chapter Seven

• • • • • • • • • • •

Flooding? Are you sure?" I ask Zoe. The image of the giant puddle in Mrs. Clark's front yard pops into my mind. "Is it actually flooding? Maybe they're just evacuating people to be safe. You know, as a precaution."

"I don't think so." Zoe shrugs. "They said it's flooding. Come see for yourself—they're not showing anything else on TV except the hurricane."

We all follow Zoe back through the door from the clinic to the house and crowd into the kitchen, almost tripping over Sneakers, who follows us and whimpers anxiously at all the commotion. Jacqueline Jermaine is on the TV, reporting from right here in Ambler. She's standing in the parking lot of the Acme supermarket, the wind whipping her usually neat hair into a wild mess.

"Jacqueline Jermaine, reporting live!" she shouts into the wind. "As you can see, we're feeling the effects of Hurricane Felix here in Ambler. Residents of Montgomery and Bucks counties are being urged to remain indoors and stay tuned for storm updates and evacuation information. People in low-lying areas should prepare for evacuation."

Brenna frowns, patting Sneakers, who has settled down on top of her feet. "I don't get it. Why would they need to evacuate here? We're not near the ocean."

"That's why." David points at the TV screen. "Look!"

The picture has switched to show a row of homes. At least I guess they're homes. All we can see are their roofs—the rest is underwater.

"That's Oakwood!" Maggie exclaims. "I recognize that gas station sign. But that's right outside of town! I can't believe it's so flooded there!"

"Shh!" I say anxiously. "I want to hear what Jacqueline Jermaine is saying."

"Too late," Zoe comments. "They're back to the anchor guy."

A few seconds later, the picture switches again, and David gasps. The camera is scanning a row of stalls with terrified horses inside. Water in the aisle outside the stalls looks like it's at least a foot deep.

The anchorman is explaining that the pictures were taken this morning at a horse show outside of Philadelphia. The fairgrounds flooded overnight, and rescue workers are trying to get the horses out.

The camera zooms in on one stall, where a gray horse is tossing his head and rearing, his eyes rolling back until the whites show. He lets out a noise that doesn't sound like it could have come from a horse at all.

"Poor guy!" Zoe says. "He's terrified. I hope they get him out of there!"

We hold our breath as we watch several people try to approach the horse and grab his halter. He keeps rearing, flailing his front hooves. Nobody can get close to him.

"Calm down, dude," David whispers, his eyes

locked on the screen. "They're just trying to help you."

"He's too scared to realize that," I say, remembering how weird Mittens, Socrates, and Stormy acted yesterday. If dogs and cats can be freaked out by a storm, I figures horses can be, too.

The horse continues to thrash around in his stall, whinnying in terror. As I watch, I feel real fear creeping over me, too. What if my father is wrong? What if my house, the clinic, our whole town is in danger from the rising waters, just like Oakwood? What would I do if I were trapped in the flood, just like that poor horse?

I turn my face away from the others. I definitely don't want my friends to think I'm scared. David might tease me again. But it's no use. I can't help thinking about Lucy. I really hope she's okay. I remember what my father said last night about Willow Street getting flooded out ten years ago, and I think about that deep puddle in Mrs. Clark's front yard.

On TV, someone finally manages to fling a towel over the horse's eyes. "Cool!" David says with relief. "A blindfold. That should help."

Sure enough, once the towel is tied over the

horse's eyes, he calms down a little. Someone leads him out of the stall and up to higher ground. We all cheer. The announcer reports that all the horses were evacuated from the fair-grounds safely.

Unfortunately, our cheer sets Sherlock howl-ing. "Yikes!" Zoe cries, clapping her hands over her ears as Sneakers lets out a startled yip. "Forget the hurricane. That dog is a natural disaster!"

"Was that the phone?" Brenna says, interrupt-ing whatever Maggie starts to say in her dog's defense.

I hurry over to the phone on the end table as David mutes the TV. The button for the clinic line is blinking. I pick up the receiver, praying that whoever is on the other end can hear me over Sherlock's howling. "Hello, Dr. Mac's Place," I say. "Can I help you?"

"Hi, this is Bill Jermaine."

"Oh! Hi," I say. "It's Sunita. Is Stormy all right?"

"I hope so." He sounds worried. "I'm rather concerned about him, actually. Is Dr. MacKenzie available?"

I clutch the phone, wondering if something

new is wrong with Stormy. Sherlock finally quiets down—thank goodness. "Um, no. Can I take a message?"

"I'd appreciate that," Bill says. "You see, I'm stuck at work because of flooding. I had planned to dash home and check on Stormy. I wanted to give him another dose of his tranquilizer and bring him inside. He's in his outdoor kennel right now. He seemed calmer there than in the house this morning, so we left him out. I should have known better. But since the clinic is so close to our house, I was hoping Dr. Mac or Gabe could go get him and look after him until I can get there. Do you think they might be able to do that?"

"Um..." I'm not sure what to say. Dr. Mac would probably agree if she were here, but she's not. And I definitely don't feel like leading that huge dog through the storm. I glance quickly at the others, who are watching me curiously. With a gulp, I remember how David teased me yesterday about being a scaredy-cat—and I remember the horse. "Yes," I tell Bill. "Don't worry. I know she'll want to help."

"Thank you, Sunita." Bill sounds relieved. "I really appreciate this. Tell Dr. Mac I'll be by as soon as I can."

"Sure. Bye." I hang up.

What have I done?

"Who was that?" Maggie asks.

After I tell them the whole story, Zoe tugs on a strand of her long blond hair and frowns. "Why didn't you tell him that Dr. Mac and Dr. Gabe are both out?" she says. "There's no telling when they'll be back to go get Stormy."

"I know," I say. "That's why we have to go get him ourselves." I'm already nervous about what I've agreed to do. But I know it was the right decision. Even though Stormy scares me a little, he's a nice dog. I hate the thought of him being trapped, like the horse we just saw on TV. What if his outdoor kennel floods or blows away or something? What if he gets struck by lightning?

"Sunita's right," Brenna says, jumping to her feet, which makes Sneakers start barking. "Come on!" she shouts over the noise. "Let's get moving!"

"Wait!" Maggie cries. "We can't all go. Someone needs to stay here in case any patients come in—and to tell Gran where we are when she gets back."

We all exchange anxious glances.

"I'll stay," Zoe speaks up after a second, bending down to soothe Sneakers. "Humidity does terrible things to my hair anyway," she jokes nervously.

• • • • • • •

We all hurry back into the clinic and put on our raincoats. Mine's still a little wet from this morning. David opens the door. Outside, the sky looks worse than ever. There are puddles everywhere, as well as tree limbs and all sorts of debris. By the time we've gone half a block, the rain finds its way into my shoes and down the back of my neck.

The wind is still blowing, and a siren is blaring somewhere nearby. We don't talk much. The Jermaines' house is only about four blocks away, on the corner of Franklin and Willow streets.

We struggle against the wind down the first block, then the second. But we keep moving. An animal needs our help, and that's the only thing on my mind. I know my friends feel the same way.

Before long we're turning on to Franklin. The Jermaines live on a block lined with nice colonial homes that have backyards overlooking the old section of town. I hear barking in the distance.

As we get closer to the Jermaines' green-and-white house at the end of the block, the barking grows louder, along with a sound of rattling metal. It's coming from behind the house.

"That's Stormy!" David says. "His kennel must be around back."

We run around the side of the house. Suddenly Brenna stops in front of us.

"What's wrong?" I ask.

Then I look past her and gasp in horror. The whole backyard is flooded under two feet of water—including Stormy's kennel!

Chapter Eight

. . . .

Stormy is hysterical with fear—he keeps bounding up onto the top of the doghouse, then slipping off and splashing down into the water. Each time, he leaps straight up as if the water is burning hot, then races forward and rebounds off the wire kennel door. Then it's back to the doghouse roof again. His ears are plastered back against his head, and his expression is panicky. His barking sounds hoarse, like he's been doing it for a long time.

Maggie hurries us forward. "We've got to get him out of there! He's freaking out—he's going to hurt himself, if he hasn't already."

Behind the house, the ground slopes down, then levels off again where Stormy's kennel is. The doghouse is an island surrounded by muddy water. We march right up to the kennel, with the water lapping at our knees.

"How are we going to get him back to the clinic?" I ask. "We don't have a leash."

"There's one." David points to a nylon leash hanging on a hook near the kennel door.

"Good eye!" Brenna shouts above Stormy's barking. "Who's going to be the brave one?"

Okay, Sunita. Don't think—just go.

I grab the leash from the kennel wall. Maggie is shouting something behind me, but I tune her out.

I flip the latch on the kennel door, fling it open, and barge inside. "Good dog," I say breathlessly, trying to make my voice calm and soothing, just like it was when I was comforting Lucy yesterday at the clinic. "It's all right, sweetie."

Stormy's barking drowns out my voice. I don't think he even sees me standing there. He's on top of the doghouse again, his claws scrabbling for a foothold on the rain-slick surface. He starts to slide off and jumps instead, splashing into two feet of muddy water on the ground.

"Calm down, Stormy, okay?" I plead, my hand clutching the leash. "I want to help you."

Stormy pushes off the side of his kennel, rebounding off the chain-link fence like a trampoline. I flinch when I see him coming straight at me. Oh, no!

"Move!" Maggie shouts. She's so close that I feel her breath on my face. She grabs the leash and pushes me toward the door. I stumble on the threshold and fall to my knees outside, splashing into the water. Glancing over my shoulder, I see Maggie standing just inside the door, looking very small beside Stormy, who has missed running into her but is still bouncing around the wire pen like crazy. How is she ever going to calm him down and get him to safety?

Maggie claps her hands and lets out a sharp whistle. Startled, Stormy freezes and looks toward her.

"Sit!" Maggie thunders, her voice louder and deeper than I've ever heard it.

The dog responds instantly, dropping onto his haunches right there in the water. He looks surprised and uncertain. Maggie doesn't give him a chance to figure out what's going on. She darts forward and quickly snaps the leash onto his collar. As soon as she does, Stormy seems to sort of go limp. His tense muscles relax, and his ears return to their normal position. In a matter of seconds, Maggie's leading him out of the kennel.

"Wow!" Brenna yells with admiration. Stormy doesn't look too happy about sloshing through the water, but he's walking meekly at Maggie's side. "That was awesome! How did you know he would listen to you?"

"I didn't," Maggie admits. "But I know he's well trained, so I gave it my best shot."

"Pretty good shooting. Or should I say shouting?" David says with a grin. He pats Stormy. "And pretty good dog."

I climb to my feet, feeling embarrassed. What was I thinking? I should have let Maggie handle it from the start.

No one says anything about my mishap, though. Brenna pushes back her brown hair, which is dripping into her eyes. "Come on," she says. "We'd better get out of here before we all float away."

We make our way toward the front of the house with Maggie and Stormy in the lead. This time we have to step around one end of the canoe that was on top of the Jermaines' van yesterday. They must have left it in the backyard, but it's floating now. Finally we're on dry ground again.

That's a relief. All that water was making me really nervous.

We head for the corner and stop to catch our breath. I can't help but look over my shoulder and down the hill at the old part of town and Willow Street.

Oh, no! Willow Street is underwater! Just a short distance away, the street slopes down and completely disappears. A block farther, the mailboxes are barely visible above the water. And by the middle of that block, the water is almost up to the second floor of the houses. Through the drizzle, I can barely see Mrs. Clark's house at the far end—there are a couple of large trees in the way—but it must be more than half submerged. Lucy...

"Do you think they've evacuated everyone already?" Maggie asks.

"Look!" Brenna cries, cutting her off.

In the distance, I see a motorboat chugging toward us. As it gets closer, I see who's inside—two men in bright yellow slickers and a small

white-haired woman wrapped in a plaid raincoat.

"Mrs. Clark!" I cry.

At that moment, Mrs. Clark spots us. "Help!"
she cries, waving her hands at us. "My poor
Lucy!"

Maggie, David, and I run toward the boat,
splashing down the hill until we're knee-deep
in water.

"Guys! Don't go out too far!" warns Brenna,
who stays back with Stormy.

"Are you okay?" I yell over the sounds of the
wind and the boat's motor. "Where's Lucy?"

"She's still in the house!" Mrs. Clark calls
back. "She was frightened by the men and the
boat. She ran and hid in the attic. They insisted
I leave her."

"I'm sorry, ma'am," one of the rescue workers says. "We couldn't spend any more time. The
water's rising quickly, and we need to get you to
the emergency shelter, which is where you kids
should be—under shelter."

I open my mouth to protest—to tell them
about Lucy's broken leg, her diabetes—but the
rescue workers are already steering the boat
toward the next street. Mrs. Clark shouts about

Lucy, but her words are drowned out by the sounds of the boat's motor.

I stare down the hill. I remember how those flooded houses looked on TV. And the flooded stable. What if it was Mittens? It all makes me feel so scared and helpless that I have to clench my hands into fists to stop them from shaking.

Then I remember how Lucy meowed at me this morning, bumping her head against my hand when I bent to pet her. And I know what I have to do.

Chapter Nine

. . . .

We've got to save her," I tell Maggie and David as we turn and walk back to Brenna and Stormy.

"You've got to be kidding," David says. "How are we supposed to do that? Build an ark?"

I frown. "This is no time for jokes. Come on, we need a plan."

Maggie shoots a worried glance down the street. "I don't know, Sunita," she says. "I mean, I want to help Lucy, too. But—"

"No buts," I interrupt firmly. "Lucy needs us. We're the only ones who can help her. We've got to do it."

Just then another big gust of wind sweeps

by, blowing away any words my friends might have tried to say. We all hold on to our hoods as Stormy lets out a brief howl.

"Whew!" David says when he can speak again. "Felix doesn't know when to let up."

"Yeah," Brenna says. "For a minute there, Stormy sounded like Sherlock."

Maggie nods. "I'm glad Sherlock is safe and sound at home," she says. "Or I would be..." Her voice trails off, and she looks at me. "Oh," she says. "You know, Sunita, you're right. If it was one of our pets in trouble, we'd do everything we could to help. Why should it be any different for Lucy? Gran never turns her back on an animal in trouble."

"Yeah," Brenna agrees slowly, glancing down the block toward Mrs. Clark's house. "And neither can we."

"Okay, I guess I'm in, too," David says with a shrug. I wonder if he's thinking about that terrified horse. "So what's our plan?"

I smile with relief. I couldn't have tried this alone. Daddy always says there's safety in numbers. "I guess we should go closer and see how it looks. Maybe we'll think of something then."

"I'll take Stormy back to the clinic," Brenna speaks up. "He'll just be in the way."

I'm glad she volunteered. I don't think I could stand to go back to the clinic without knowing whether Lucy was safe.

Brenna tugs on Stormy's leash. The big dog's tail is still between his legs, but he's not whining anymore. In fact, he looks a little braver now that he's away from his kennel and the standing water.

"Good luck," Brenna says. "I'll tell Dr. Mac what's going on if she's back. Maybe she can send help." With a quick wave, she hurries off toward the clinic, chattering cheerfully to Stormy as she goes.

"Now what?" Maggie asks, glancing at me.

I realize that she and David are counting on me to come up with a plan. I stare at the flooded street, trying to figure out what to do now. How do we get to Mrs. Clark's house? The road slopes down so steeply that most of it is totally underwater. The lower half of the block where Mrs. Clark's house is looks like the street on Oakwood that we saw on TV—just roofs.

"The river and the creeks must have overflowed their banks and mixed with the rain," Maggie says. "This street is probably the lowest point in town."

David shakes his head. "That area over by the park is lower than this."

"Maybe," Maggie agrees. "I forgot about that."

I can't believe they're standing around debating where the flooding is worse. The only important thing is what we're going to do about it. "You guys—Lucy!" I remind them. "We have to rescue her!"

Maggie glances at the half-submerged houses. "Um, okay," she says slowly. "But I'm still not sure how. Mrs. Clark's house is probably in seven to eight feet of water."

"Can we swim over?" David suggests.

I gulp. I can feel my face start to turn red.

Before I can speak, Maggie shakes her head. "It's not safe," she says. "It's pretty far—and there's no telling what kind of stuff is in the water. You could swim right into a mailbox without even knowing it's there."

I can't help feeling relieved. "Maybe if we go around the back..." I begin.

"Uh-uh." David shakes his head. "I've been

back there behind those houses. There's sort of a canyon—it'll be even deeper back there."

I bite my lip. We have to act fast. It's pouring again, and the waters are rising quickly. If we don't rescue Lucy soon, the whole house will be underwater. There's no way she can save herself. "There has to be a way," I say, feeling a little desperate.

Maggie sighs, staring out across the water. "Maybe we should go back to the clinic," she suggests uncertainly. "Gran or Dr. Gabe must be back by now. They'll know what to do to help Lucy."

"Sounds good to me," David agrees. "There's no sense hanging around here any longer. Because the only way we could possibly reach Lucy now is in a—"

"Canoe!" I shout.

"That's it! The Jermaines have a canoe in their yard," David adds.

"What are we waiting for?" Maggie yells.

"Now you two will be able to prove who's a better canoer," I say, running back up the hill toward the Jermaines' house.

The canoe is right where I remember. It's a lot heavier than it looks, though.

"Maybe we should dump out these life jackets," David says.

"No!" I say a little too quickly. Maggie and David blink at me in surprise. "Um, I mean, let's put them on. Better safe than sorry."

The others shrug and do as I suggest. I strap my vest on carefully. It makes me feel braver—a little bit, at least.

We turn the canoe upside down and rest the yoke on our shoulders. We can move it only a few feet at a time, even with all three of us carrying it. Soon my shoulder muscles are aching, and my hands are numb from gripping the edge of the canoe. The half block to the water's edge seems more like a mile.

Finally the water starts splashing over our shoes. We lower the canoe to the ground and shove it through the shallow part of the floodwaters until it starts to float. David grabs the line tied to the front end and holds it steady as Maggie clambers aboard.

I still can't stop worrying about Lucy. I hope she's not trying to escape. With her broken leg, she won't be able to swim very far. Besides that, she needs her insulin injections to control her diabetes.

"Go ahead, Sunita," David says. "I'll hold it while you get in."

I look at the canoe. It bobs in the little waves the wind is making in the water. Then I stare down at the muddy water, feeling queasy and scared. "Um, maybe one of us should stay here," I say. "That way I can run for help if you guys get into any trouble."

David blinks at me in surprise. "What?" he says. "But the canoe's plenty big enough for three people."

"Yeah, but you guys are the great canoers, remember?" I add. "Now go ahead! Lucy's waiting for you."

"Okay, okay," David says, splashing out and vaulting into the canoe. He picks up the second paddle, and soon he and Maggie have the long, slim boat moving away from me.

I collapse against a blue mailbox on the wet sidewalk, watching them go. They're shouting to each other—I can hear them over the water. But the words don't really sink in. I picture Lucy alone in her house, scared and confused.

The rain is coming down so hard now that I lose sight of the canoe after just a few minutes. I can barely make out the outline of Mrs. Clark's house. I peer toward it, wondering what's happening.

● ● ● ● ● ● ●

After what seems to be the longest fifteen minutes of my life, I finally make out the shape of the canoe returning. Crossing my fingers, I wait for it to get closer.

"Did you get her?" I call when Maggie and David are finally in shouting range.

They don't answer. They're paddling hard, and I can see that their expressions are grim. And I don't see a blue-eyed Siamese anywhere.

My heart drops like a stone.

Chapter Ten

• • • • • • • • • • • •

I don't even realize that I've waded out into the flooded area until I feel the water lapping at my knees. I grab the rope David tosses to me and help pull the canoe up into the shallow water. "What happened?" I ask, my heart in my throat.

"We saw her," Maggie says breathlessly, wiping water out of her eyes. She's soaked! "Lucy was sitting by the attic window meowing her head off. But we couldn't get close enough to it in the boat—there are these big trees in the way."

David nods. "Maggie swam over to the window and tried to get her," he adds. "But Lucy ran away and hid when Maggie opened the window and tried to grab her."

"I climbed into the attic through the window," Maggie says. "But I couldn't find her. And she wouldn't come when I called."

"Oh, no," I whisper. "Now what are we going to do?"

There's only one answer. I gulp as I realize it.

"We have to try again," I say, trying to sound brave enough though my knees are shaking and my guts are quivering. "This time I'll come along. Lucy knows me—I'm sure I can coax her out if anyone can."

Maggie nods and exchanges a glance with David. "That's what we thought, too."

They don't say it, but I can tell they're wishing I'd just come along in the first place. I can't explain to them why I couldn't—I don't want to admit the truth. What would they think if they knew? I'm just glad they're willing to go out and try again, even though they're probably even colder and wetter and more exhausted than I am.

Taking a deep breath, I wade over to the canoe and climb in. David and Maggie push the boat out with their paddles, and I hold my breath as it starts to float. I've been on boats before, but this is different. It's a lot smaller, for one thing. The water looks awfully close—especially since an inch or so of water is sloshing around in the bottom of the canoe. I'm not sure if it's from the rain that's still falling steadily or from water splashing over the sides. Either way, I'm glad I'm still wearing my bright orange life vest.

"Let's go," Maggie says, digging in deeply with her paddle.

I sit as still as possible in the center seat of the rocking and swaying canoe, trying to stay out of the way as my friends paddle. The water slides by as the canoe cuts forward, heading deeper and deeper into the flood zone. Is this a big mistake? I wince as a large floating branch bounces off the side of the canoe with a clunk. My whole body feels numb, and I want to shout for my friends to turn back. I'm not sure I can do this after all.

But I bite my tongue. I have to try, for Lucy's sake. By the time other help arrives, it could be too late. I would never forgive myself if something happened to Lucy because I was too scared to try to save her.

I stare grimly ahead as my friends paddle,

clutching the sides of the boat and trying not to look down at the water swirling all around us. How deep is it? I don't even want to know.

David begins to whistle quietly. Maggie joins in. Soon I join in, too. It helps take my mind off Lucy.

Mrs. Clark's house looms closer ahead. I can hardly believe how different it looks now compared to early this morning. It's amazing and scary that the water could rise so fast. Now those statistics I read about on the Internet are making a lot more sense.

"Mrrwowrr!"

The familiar cry comes during a brief lull in the wind. "Lucy!" I exclaim, momentarily forgetting everything else, even my own fear. I squint into the rain and spot a flash of movement at the small window just beneath the peak of the roof. "I see her! She's in the attic window!"

"Yeah," Maggie says. "That's where we saw her before."

Another loud Siamese meow reaches our ears before the sounds of Hurricane Felix swallow it. David and Maggie are paddling faster now. "Almost there," David pants. "Last time we

pulled right up to that big branch and tied the
boat there while Maggie swam."

I look ahead. A tree emerges from the water,
stretching taller than the houses around it. I
never really noticed the tree before—usually its
spreading branches are way over my head, shad-
ing Mrs. Clark's front yard and the roof of her
house. But now that we're eight feet higher than
usual, thanks to the flood, I see that several large
branches stretch out in every direction, blocking
our path to the front of the house.

"Are you sure we can't get the canoe through
there?" I scan the water between us and the
house, praying for an opening to appear.

David shakes his head. "Believe me, we tried."
He sticks his paddle in the water, steering us a
little closer to the largest branch, which is about
fifteen feet from the attic window. "And we can't
go around to the other side of the house. There
are more trees in the backyard, so we'll have the
same problem."

"But don't worry. This branch isn't that far
from the house, see?" Maggie says, reaching
over the side of the canoe and grabbing the large,
sturdy branch, helping David pull us alongside.

"All you have to do is climb out onto the branch and jump into the water on the other side."

I feel my whole body go numb again. Now what? I can't keep my secret from them any longer.

"Well, there's just one problem." I gulp, not daring to meet their eyes. "I—I can't swim."

Chapter Eleven

. . . .

What?" Maggie stares at me in disbelief.

David blinks. "Wait a minute," he says, shaking his head. "You can't swim? Since when?"

"Since always." I can tell my face is bright red, but I continue. "I've always been afraid of the water. I dropped out of beginner swimming lessons at the YMCA."

"Wow," Maggie says. "Now what are we going to do?"

David chews on his lower lip. "I could swim over," he offers. "Maybe—"

"Forget it," Maggie cuts him off. "If Lucy wouldn't come to me, she won't come to you, either. This is hopeless. We should get help. Gran will know what to do."

Glancing at the house, I almost agree with her. It would be so much easier to give up and wait for help. Brenna is probably on her way back with reinforcements right now.

Then Lucy meows again. She tips forward a little, sliding her front feet toward the water lapping below the window, as if she's thinking about jumping. She wobbles on her splinted fore-leg. I suck in my breath, sure that she's going to fall in.

She catches herself just in time and backs up, letting out another desperate meow. I gulp, try-ing to swallow my terror. "I'll go," I blurt before I lose my nerve. "I mean, I'm wearing a life vest. Even if I don't know how to swim, I should be able to paddle over there and get her."

Maggie looks uncertain. "Are you sure?"

"It's the only way." I try to sound confident. It's not easy, since my insides feel like they've all suddenly turned to Jell-O.

I kick off my shoes. David grabs the rope that's coiled up in the front part of the boat. One end is tied to a ring at the front of the canoe. "We can tie this to your vest," David suggests. "That way we can make sure you don't get carried away by the current."

"Maybe we can even help you steer a little," Maggie adds.

I nod and scoot around on the narrow canoe seat so that they can tie the rope to the back of my vest. David crouches behind me. I can't see what he's doing, but after a moment, I feel a tug on the life vest.

"There," he says. "That should do it."

"Ready?" Maggie asks.

I nod. I don't trust my voice to speak. Taking a deep breath, I clutch the edge of the boat with both hands and stare down at the water. Can I do this?

I have to do this. I don't let myself think about it anymore, and I climb out of the canoe onto the large branch. It feels solid and comforting under my feet. Then I slide down into the water, push off, and let go.

∙ ∙ ∙ ∙ ∙ ∙ ∙

The water is a lot colder than I expected. And it's moving around more than I realized, too, making me feel like one of Harshil's toy boats bobbing in the bathtub. My vest doesn't hold me up as much as I thought it would—I'm so low in the water that when a little wave comes toward me, it washes right over my head. For a second, I'm totally underwater! I forget to hold my breath, and take in a mouthful of water. There's a weird sort of roaring sound in my ears.

I thrash around until I pop up above the surface and can breathe again. I shake my head to get my hair out of my eyes. I cough and spit out water. It tastes disgusting. I try not to think of all the germs I probably just swallowed. I have enough to worry about right now.

"Are you okay?" David calls.

I can't answer him. I'm too busy trying to spit wet hair out of my mouth without losing track of what my arms and legs are doing. Every time I let my muscles relax, it feels like I'm going to sink straight down into the water. So I keep my limbs moving around, trying to imitate what I've seen other people do while they're swimming. With the help of my life vest, it seems to work pretty well.

"Yeah," I gasp. "I'm okay."

"Don't worry," David calls. "If you get too scared, just yell, and we'll pull you back in with the rope."

I don't want to waste any energy answering, so I just nod. Then I turn around to face Mrs. Clark's house.

Okay, Sunita, I tell myself firmly. *Time to swim.*

I think back to a hot, sunny day a few weeks ago. It was a slow day at the clinic, so at lunchtime, Dr. Gabe took us to the park for a picnic. Sherlock came, too, and while we were eating, he waded out into the pond for a swim. If you've never seen a basset hound swim, I can tell you it's not a pretty sight. But he managed to get around pretty well, paddling energetically with his stubby front paws.

As I try to imitate Sherlock's swimming style, I see another ripple coming toward me. Not wanting to let my head go underwater again, I thrash harder with my arms to raise myself up in the water. The tiny wave washes by, splashing my chin. But my head stays up. I smile with triumph.

"Hey! Sunita!" Maggie yells from behind me. "Kick with your legs!"

I do as she says. I'm focusing so much on my legs that I forget about my arms for a second. I remember them when I feel my face sink-ing lower into the water. Finally I have all four limbs working at the same time. That does the trick. Mrs. Clark's house starts to get closer. Of course, that means the canoe must be getting farther away behind me. But I try not to think about that.

"Mrrwowrr!" Lucy's voice floats out across the water.

I glance up at the frightened cat, blinking the water out of my eyes. She's perched in the window. The rain makes it hard to see clearly, but it looks like she's watching me. The water is lapping at the house just a foot or so beneath the windowsill.

I have to do this—for Lucy. I kick harder, aiming straight for the window. The house is only about six feet away now. If I were on dry land, it would hardly seem like any distance at all. But right now, it seems as wide as the Mississippi River—or maybe the Atlantic Ocean.

I can see Lucy sitting there watching me, and that gives me the strength to keep going. When my fingers brush against the brick wall, I feel like cheering. Instead, I grab the edge of the windowsill. The window is open, and there's no screen. Lucy jumps off the windowsill and back into the attic.

"Mrrrr?" she says uncertainly, rubbing the top of her head on an old trunk. When I peek in the window, I'm happy to see that the floor is still dry.

"It's okay, sweetie," I say breathlessly. I try to keep my voice as calm and soothing as I can as I climb in through the window. It feels good to stand on something solid again. "Don't worry, Lucy. It's me, Sunita. I want to get you out of here."

The cat crouches down, her eyes trained on my face. The tip of her tail switches back and forth. I can tell she's still nervous and trying to decide what to do. Maybe she doesn't recognize me with wet, stringy hair.

I look around for the cat carriers Mrs. Clark mentioned yesterday. Even though it's the middle of the day, it's dark in the attic. The power is out, and only a little grayish daylight comes in through the window. But I soon spot not one, but two hard plastic cat carriers stacked neatly by the wall. Remembering Mittens' hiding place at home, I grab the smaller of the two. Maybe being in a small place will help Lucy feel more secure.

Lucy jumps when I pick up the carrier. She turns and races off, moving surprisingly fast despite her splint. She disappears behind some cardboard boxes.

Shoot, Sunita. You know Lucy always runs as soon as a carrier comes into sight!

"Lucy!" I exclaim. "Come on, girl! I'm here to help you."

I wish we were all safe and sound, back on dry land again. Taking a deep breath, I force myself to calm down. I have to be patient.

Crouching down beside the cat carrier, I carefully swing the door open, trying not to make any scary noises. "It's okay, baby," I croon, watching the spot where Lucy disappeared. "I know all that water out there is scary. I don't like it any more than you do, believe me. But I couldn't just leave you here by yourself. I'm here to help you. Now you need to help me by being a good kitty and letting me get you out of here."

I keep talking, saying whatever comes into my head. Finally I see her nose poke out from behind the boxes. She stares at me, her whiskers twitching.

Still talking softly, I ease forward inch by inch. Lucy watches me nervously, but she doesn't move.

"Come on, sweetie," I croon, holding out my hand. "Come here, Lucy girl."

Lucy crouches lower, looking suspicious. I'm afraid she's going to dart away and hide somewhere among the boxes and old suitcase in the attic.

"Listen," I whisper to her. "I'm scared of water. You're scared of water. But I'm here now, and I really want to get you out of this place before the water gets in. Believe me, you'll be glad when we're both back on dry land." I clear my throat, trying not to think about the floodwaters swirling around the house. "I'll be glad, too."

Lucy seems to be listening to me. Her large, dark ears are pricked toward me, and she doesn't back away as I continue to inch forward.

Finally I'm closer enough to reach out and grab her gently by the scruff of the neck. I wouldn't normally pick up an adult cat that way, but since I can use only one hand. I figure it's safer than trying to grab her any other way—especially with her broken leg.

Lucy struggles, but I hold on tightly, lifting her

carefully with my other hand supporting most of her weight. She gives me a few scratches with her claws, but I hardly notice. Soon she's safely locked in the cat carrier.

"Whew!" I say. "Now what do you say we get out of here, okay?"

I blink, wondering exactly how we're going to do that. How am I supposed to get the cat carrier back out to the canoe?

Then I realize the answer. I pick up the carrier and carry it to the window. David and Maggie are watching from the canoe. I give them a thumbs-up to let them know I have Lucy. Then I swing up onto the windowsill before reaching back into the attic for the carrier.

When David sees me lowering the cat carrier toward the water, he shouts out in alarm. "What are you doing?" he cries. "She'll drown!"

"Don't worry," I call back breathlessly. "It'll float."

I hope I'm right. I'm remembering what I learned last year in science class about buoyancy. That's another word for how well things float. And I learned that a lightweight, hollow object with a solid bottom—like a canoe or a plastic cat carrier—has a lot of buoyancy. I just have to keep the door and airholes above water.

I hold my breath as the carrier sinks slightly, then bobs back to the surface, floating easily. Some water has splashed in, and Lucy yowls in protest.

"Don't be scared," I whisper, hardly daring to believe I've actually done it. "You'll be safe now. Don't worry," I turn and wave to let Maggie and David know that we're coming. I see David start swimming toward me, and hear the faint sound of Maggie cheering from the canoe.

Soon David is there beside me. "Good job, Sunita," he cries happily. "You did it!"

I grin tiredly as he starts swimming back, pushing the carrier—and a very noisy Lucy—along with him. A second later, I feel a tug on the back of my vest. With relief, I remember the rope. I push off from the windowsill, letting Maggie pull me back toward the canoe. I do my best to help her by paddling, although my arms and legs feel like they have lead weights attached to them. I've never been so tired in my life.

But I'm happy. Lucy is safe!

Chapter Twelve

• • • • • • • • • • •

There you are!" Dr. Mac shouts when Maggie, David, and I enter the clinic twenty minutes later. "Thank goodness! Gabe just went out searching for you."

She looks sort of angry but also very relieved. Zoe is sitting at the reception desk when we come in, but she hops up and rushes over. "Wow," she says, handing us each a towel. "You guys look like you went through the washing machine."

"Yeah," David says with a grin, peeling off his raincoat. "But the dryer was broken."

Dr. Mac doesn't look amused. "You all have a lot of explaining to do," she says sternly. "But first things first." She bends over and peers into the cat carrier I'm holding. "Bring her back."

We all follow Dr. Mac into the exam room. I gently set the carrier on the examining table and peer inside at Lucy. "You're safe now, girl," I reassure her. "Just like I promised."

"So what happened, anyway?" Zoe asks curiously, leaning over to peek in at Lucy. "Brenna said the street was totally flooded. How did you rescue her?"

"Later," Dr. Mac says firmly. "We have work to do."

She opens the carrier door. I can tell that Lucy is glad to get out of there. She lets out a loud, disgruntled meow and tries to launch herself off the edge of the table—splint and all.

Dr. Mac catches her and returns her to the center of the table as David quickly grabs the carrier and moves it out of the way. "Okay, old girl," Dr. Mac murmurs, stroking Lucy gently. "Let's see what we have here. Sunita, could you bring me a clean towel, please?"

I do as she says, then watch as she carefully dries off the damp cat. Lucy starts purring, and Dr. Mac smiles.

"Sounds like she's not feeling too terribly

despite her adventure," she comments as she looks Lucy over, checking her gums and listening to her heartbeat. "There are no signs of shock or serious stress, but we'll check her glucose level just in case. Otherwise, the rainwater bath doesn't seem to have hurt her any. But I think I'll put a new splint on her, since this one might be wet inside. Sunita?"

I start setting up the splinting equipment as Dr. Mac quickly draws blood for the glucose test. By the time she finishes checking the blood, I have everything ready. Even though Lucy is awake this time, the procedure goes quickly. The cat seems tired from the day's commotion and doesn't move as Dr. Mac carefully peels away the damp bandages and removes the splint underneath. Soon her leg is neatly splinted and wrapped again.

"Good girl, Lucy," I tell her when it's all over, scratching her under her chin.

"Her sugar level is fine, and her leg is none the worse for wear," Dr. Mac tells us as she peels off her gloves. "You can go ahead and take her to the recovery room, Sunita. I'm going to call the emergency shelter and see if Mrs. Clark is there. I want to let her know that Lucy is fine and that we can keep her here for a couple of days if necessary."

"Lucy won't be the only one," Zoe comments as Dr. Mac hurries out of the room. "People have been bringing animals in all day. Did you know the human shelter won't let pets in?"

"Uh-huh," I say, too tired and relieved to explain how I know. I pick up Lucy, being careful not to jostle her new splint too much. The others tag along as I take her into the recovery room. Everyone helps to get her settled in one of the empty cages.

When we come out of the recovery room, we run into Brenna in the hall. She's leading Stormy on a leash. "Hey! I heard you made it back. How's Lucy?" she asks.

We tell her what Dr. Mac said. Meanwhile, Stormy sits at Brenna's side, gazing at her adoringly. "Looks like you made a new friend," David comments.

Brenna grins. "I tried to put him in the kennel when we got here, but he wanted to stay with me," she said. "I guess he's happy I saved him from all that wet stuff outside." She leans down to pat the big dog. "Just kidding, boy. You were totally brave on the way home."

Zoe rolls her eyes. "It's probably just as well he's out," she comments. "It's not like we have that many cages to spare."

I see what she means when we enter the kennel. It's packed with pets. All I smell is wet dog. "Wow," I say. "Were all these animals stranded by the hurricane?"

"All these and more," Zoe says. "Dr. Mac says that all the vets in the area are taking in as many pets as they can."

Luckily, there's still one large kennel available. Brenna puts Stormy in it. He starts whining immediately, then lets out a loud, sharp bark.

Brenna winces. "See?" she asks. "How about if we hang out in here for a few minutes? That might help him settle down."

"Okay," Maggie says, sitting down cross-legged near the kennel. She glances at me as I sit down next to her. "By the way, Sunita, I wanted to tell you. That was pretty cool—what you did back there."

"Yeah," David agrees. He glances at Zoe and Brenna with a grin. "You should've seen her. She was amazing."

"We make a good team," I say shyly.

Remembering how Zoe and Brenna did their part to help out, I add, "All of us."

"Yeah, we do." Maggie smiles. "But you're still the hero of the day, Sunita." David nods.

I'm not sure why they're making such a big deal out of what I did. After all, if I'd known how to swim in the first place, the whole rescue would have been a lot easier. Still, I can't help feeling proud of myself. It feels great to know that I helped to save Lucy, even though I couldn't have done it without my friends. I feel proud of all of us for rescuing Stormy.

Zoe and Brenna look a little confused. "What exactly happened?" Brenna asks, sticking her fingers through the mesh kennel door so that Stormy can lick them. "How did you get Lucy out of the house? We heard it was totally flooded over there."

"Yeah," Zoe adds. "On TV they said Willow Street was flooded with, like, eight feet of water."

David starts to tell them the story. When he gets to the part where he and Maggie go out in the canoe without me, Brenna looks confused again.

"Wait a minute," she says. "Why didn't you take Sunita with you? Lucy loves her—she could catch her a lot easier than you guys."

The cat's already out of the bag. I might as well tell them. "I never learned to swim," I explain. "So I was afraid to go out there in all that water."

"Oh!" Zoe looks at me curiously. "So then what happened?"

Maggie takes over the story and describes how she and David tried to rescue Lucy themselves. "Finally we just gave up," she goes on. "We were going to come back here for help. But then Sunita decided she would try."

David jumps in again, waving his arms around dramatically as he describes the rescue. I'm happy that he leaves out a few things—like how I almost drowned when I first jumped in, or how I swam like a basset hound. By the time he finishes, Zoe and Brenna look impressed.

"You mean you jumped in and swam to the rescue, even though you didn't know how to swim?" Zoe says, gazing at me. "That's pretty brave!"

I shrug uncertainly. "Not really," I admit. "I was totally terrified the whole time."

"So what?" Zoe says. "You still went ahead and did it."

Brenna nods. "My parents always say that's what real bravery is," she says. "It's doing something you need to do even if you're scared."

I've never thought about it that way before. But it makes sense.

Just then Stormy starts scratching at the cage door and whining. "Maybe he needs to go out," Maggie says.

Brenna lets the big dog out of his cage. I feel so happy about the way this day has turned out that I actually lean forward and pat him gently on the back as he walks by. Now that I've faced something that really scares me, it seems almost silly to be nervous about big dogs, especially ones that I know are perfectly nice and friendly.

Maybe I am a lot braver than I thought I was.

In any case, I know one thing for sure. As soon as the hurricane is over, I'm signing up for swimming lessons!

Don't Leave Your Best Friend Behind

By J.J. MACKENZIE, D.V.M.

Wild World News—Nobody is ever completely prepared for a hurricane, tornado, or earthquake to strike. That's why these events are called natural disasters.

During weather emergencies people are often asked to leave their homes. And contrary to what some people may tell you, it's not a good idea to leave your pets behind during an evacuation. If your home isn't safe for you, it's not safe for your animals, either. There are things you can do, however, to make sure you and your pets come through even the worst weather emergency safely.

PET PLAN

Don't wait until you hear the tornado sirens go off or see a hurricane on the weather report to start thinking about how to keep your pet safe. Plan ahead for your pet just as you would do for yourself. If your family already practices fire drills—which is definitely a good idea!—take a few more minutes to make a plan to handle whatever types of weather disasters are possible in your area. Decide which family member will be responsible for which duty, and go over the plan regularly so that you don't forget.

PLAN AHEAD FOR YOUR PET JUST AS YOU WOULD DO FOR YOURSELF.

NO PETS ALLOWED

In an emergency, Red Cross shelters cannot accept animals (except guide dogs for the blind and other recognized service dogs). It's better to figure out ahead of time where you and your pet can take shelter together. The best option is to plan to stay with animal-loving friends or relatives outside of the area likely to be affected by the disaster. You may also want to investigate pet-friendly hotels and motels, as well as boarding kennels that could take in your pet in an emergency. Have several options in mind in case your first choice is full or can't be reached. And don't wait until the last minute to evacuate. You won't want to be trapped in the disaster area. If rescue crews have to bring you out, they may not be able to rescue your pets as well.

EMERGENCY KIT

If you do need to evacuate with your pets, you should have an emergency kit ready to take with you quickly. It should be stored in a convenient location and packed so that you can carry it easily. Here is a list of important items to include in your kit:

1. For dogs—a collar that fits snugly, or better yet, a harness, which may give you more control over your dog in an uncertain situation. Consider a muzzle if your dog is to be boarded with animals where things are likely to get stressful. Your dog should be wearing a current license on his collar.

2. For cats and other small pets—a lightweight carrying crate.

3. Copies of your pets' health records, as well as current rabies tags. If your pet has any medical problems that require special handling or treatment, this information also should be included in the records or on the pet's collar. It's a good idea to seal your pet's records in a watertight container or plastic bag.

4. A recent photo of each pet. If your pet has any distinguishing marks, such as a kinked tail or an unusually shaped spot, be sure that they're visible on the photo. You may also want to consider having your pet tattooed or fitted with a microchip so that she can be identified even if she is separated from you without ID tags. This can be helpful even in a nonemergency situation. Ask your vet for more information.

5. A week's supply of food. Don't forget to include a can opener if you are using canned food.

6. A week's supply of clean water. Sometimes in an emergency, human water supplies can become contaminated. Fresh water for your pet may be hard to find if you don't pack it yourself.

7. At least **a week's supply of any special medications your pet may need.**

8. A litter box and kitty litter, or a pooper-scooper and plastic bags.

9. A pet first-aid kit.

10. If you will be evacuating to a known address, such as a relative's home, you can make up **temporary ID tags** with that address on them.

11. A favorite toy or other familiar item to help your pet feel at home away from home.

PET STRESS

Be prepared for your pet's behavior to change during an emergency. Have you ever noticed how your calm, purring lap cat turns into a tiger at the vet's office? Or how your friendly, people-loving dog cowers in the corner? Like a trip to the vet, a natural disaster may bring out the worst in the best-behaved pet.

Even if your pet is usually sweet and perfectly trustworthy, he may panic and try to run away or hide. He may even try to bite or scratch you if he feels threatened enough. That's why it's so important to have proper restraining devices—crates, harnesses, or collars—ready in case of emergency

THE BUDDY SYSTEM

In case you're not at home when disaster strikes, work out an emergency plan with a pet-friendly neighbor. Ideally, your emergency buddy should be someone your pet knows and trusts. Give your buddy a copy of your pet's medical records, and tell him or her where your emergency kit is stored. If your pet has a favorite hiding place where she goes when she's nervous, make sure your buddy knows that, too. You should also file a permission slip at your vet's office, allowing your buddy to authorize treatment in case your pet is injured or becomes sick. Be ready to return the favor by offering to do the same for your buddy's pet or pets.